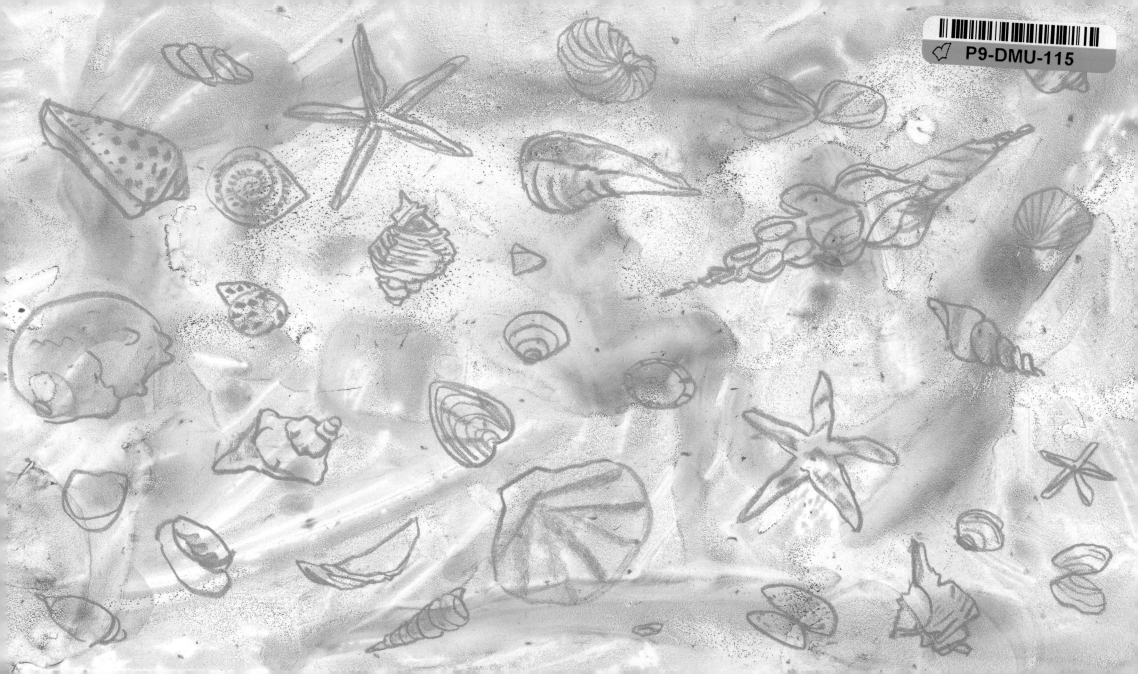

The illustrations in this book were rendered in charcoal
and acrylics and digitally manipulated.
Manufactured in China
ISBN 978-0-8118-5924-0

Library of Congress Cataloging-in-Publication Data available.

20 19 18

Chronicle Books LLC
680 Second Street, San Francisco, California 94107

www.chroniclekids.com

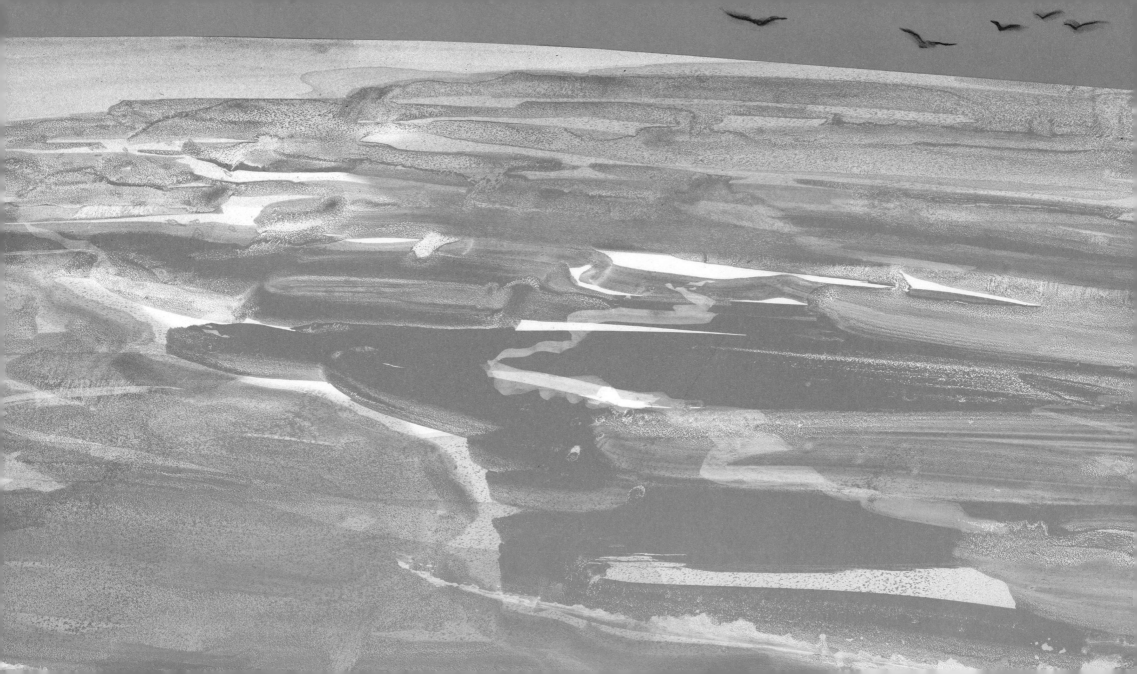

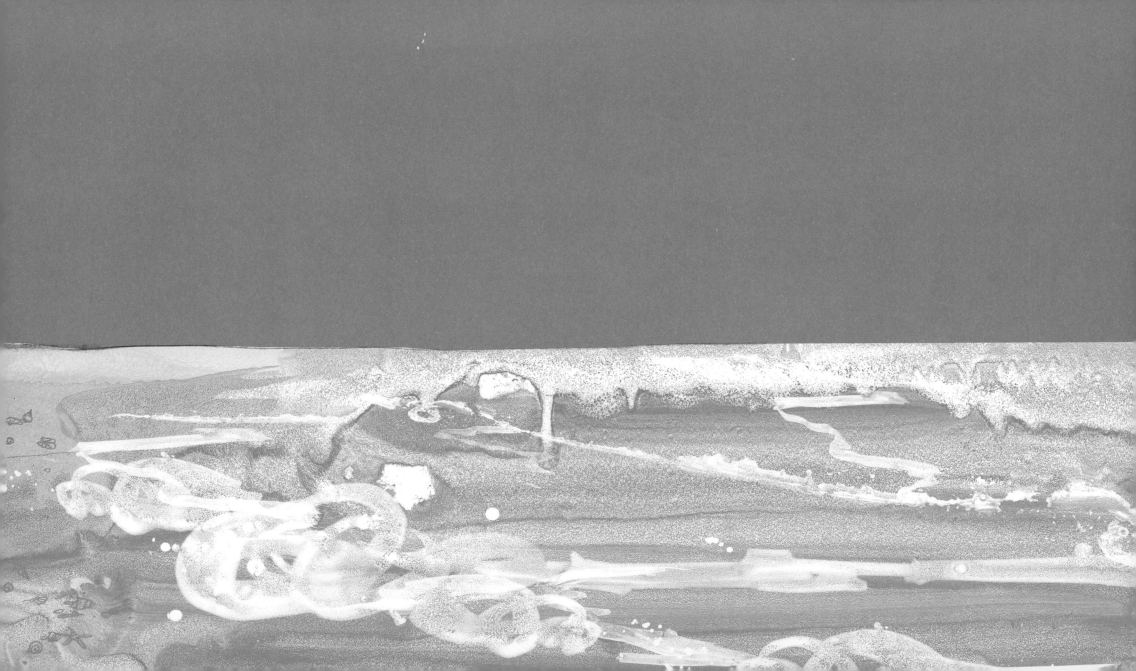

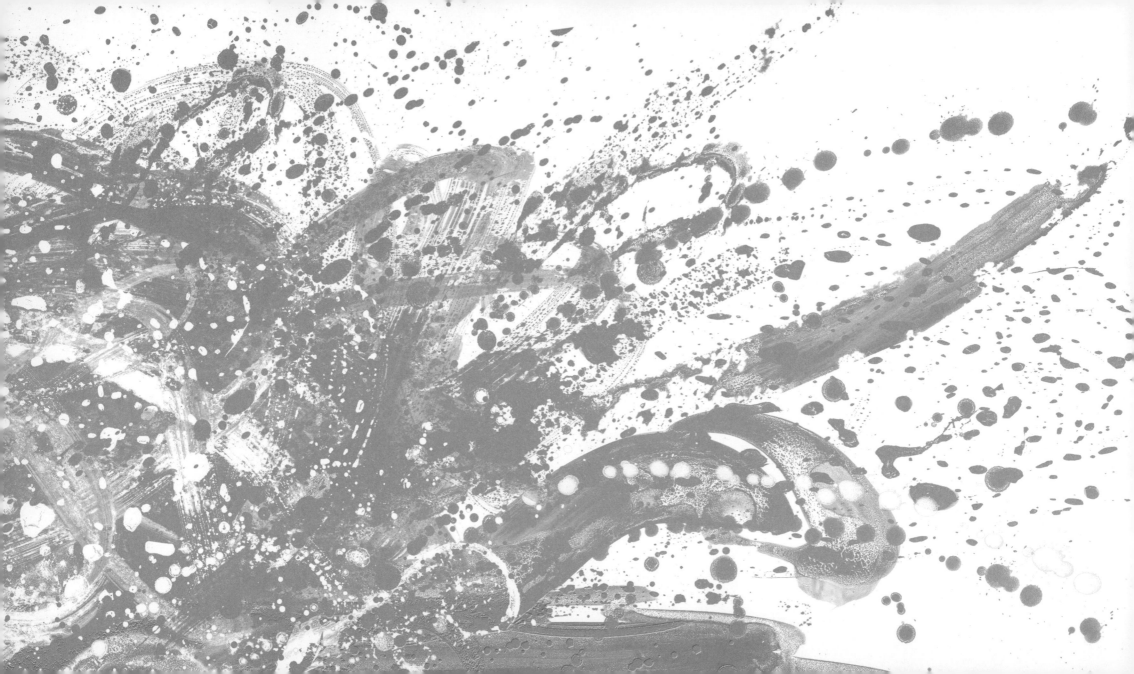

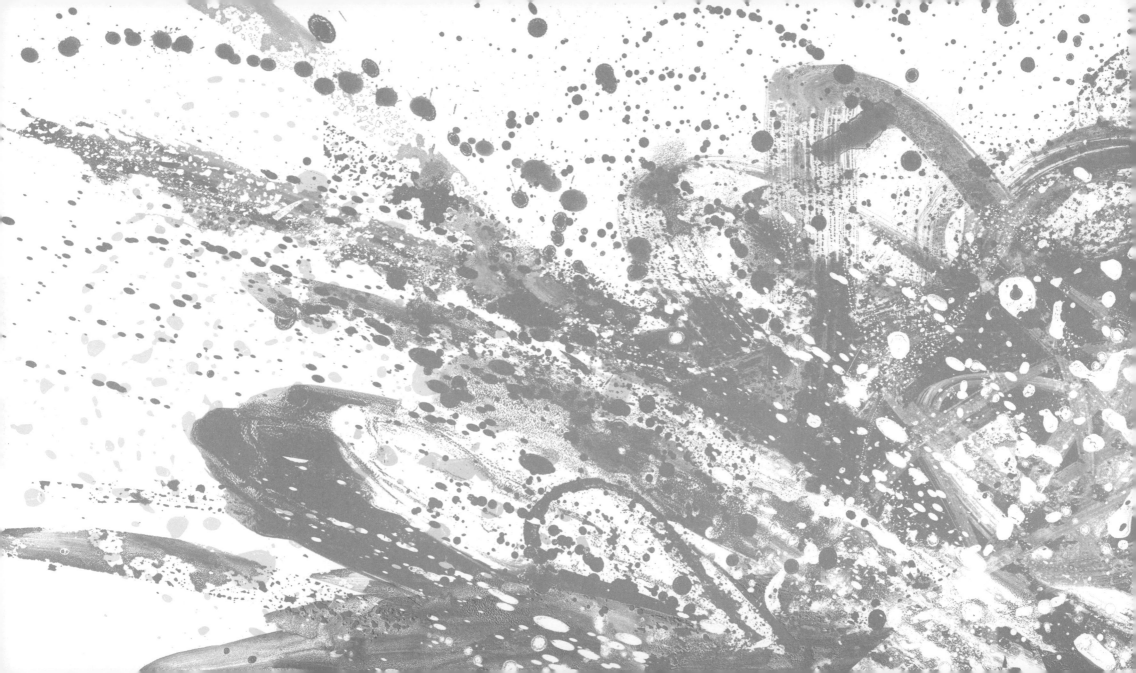

Suzy Lee

chronicle books · san francisco

For Sahn, my newborn baby —S. L.